His Forever Princess

Cowboy Fairytales

Lacy Williams

Chapter One

Once a Navy SEAL, always a SEAL.

But Gideon Hale wasn't a young and foolhardy warrior anymore.

It was early summer, but an inch of snow had covered the road through the Rocky Mountains of Colorado—a road that was more of a track than anything else.

The remote cabin stood empty and had been for months, judging by the dust covering every surface.

It didn't matter if there was an inch of dust accumulated on the countertops. That it was cold outside and getting colder. There was no room for him to be complacent, not when the princess had nearly been killed.

His wife.

His wife had nearly been killed.

He held a 9mm at the ready as he moved on stealthy feet across the cabin. It belonged to an old friend and there wasn't much to it. Not many places to hide. Maybe the curtained-off lower shelf beneath the minuscule kitchen counters. Gideon swept it aside with his foot. Empty.

He heard a soft sigh behind him as he bypassed the bed and headed for the only other door in the place. A bathroom? He nudged open the door, 9mm pointed ahead of him. Careful.

Alessandra's next sigh carried a hint of impatience. Or maybe exasperation.

He didn't stop. Couldn't. His need to keep her safe was primal.

It was also the only thing holding back the fury pounding through his veins.

He swept aside the shower curtain. For one microsecond, the motion cast a shadow on the wall. He almost pulled the trigger.

But good sense prevailed.

He turned back to the room. "Clear."

Alessandra, in her charcoal sweater over dark-colored jeans, ignored him. He'd insisted she wear a hat to cover her golden hair, but she'd taken it off sometime in the last hours driving the empty mountain roads. Now she stared out the bank of floor-to-ceiling windows.

Neither one of them had slept in almost forty-eight hours, but he wouldn't have guessed it by looking at her. She looked as regal as ever. Perfect posture, every strand of hair in place, a hint of disdain in the slight frown she wore. Disdain for their accommodations? Or because she was stuck here with him?

He didn't let the thought land. Couldn't afford the distraction.

Yet he couldn't stop his memory from shifting to provide him a glimpse of Alessandra when he'd first met her. She'd been on the run then, too. Not dressed for the weather, pale and terrified. And beautiful.

He blinked away the memory that felt like a punch.

He secured his gun into the holster at his hip and crossed to the windows, where he began lowering the blinds.

Alessandra shifted. He didn't hold out hope that she would argue with him. It had been the silent treatment ever since they'd left the Triple H's ranch house. She'd argued then, on a video call with her sister, the Queen, and a security team from the palace in Glorvaird.

Gideon and Alessandra's sister Eloise rarely got along, but this time Eloise had agreed with his plan. Which meant Gideon had overridden Alessandra's protests about this plan. Twice.

She'd iced him out since.

When he reached above his head to pull the cord for the upper blind, the bullet-wound in his side screamed against the movement.

He ignored the pain.

These windows were a direct invitation for a sniper to take an easy shot.

"You can wash up, if you'd like," he told her.

He didn't look over to see whether or not Alessandra moved. They'd only stopped when the SUV had needed gas. And each time Gideon had followed her to the bathroom. It hadn't been a trip fit for a princess. But he didn't care. This was the only way to keep her safe.

Especially since she'd left him in the dark about the threats against her.

He was so angry his hands shook. They hadn't been on the same continent since Maggie's wedding. Before that, it had been at least five years.

She didn't need him. She'd made that perfectly clear years ago. But that didn't stop him from video conferencing with her security team once a week. He always knew where she'd be. What legislation or trade agreement she was working on. The threats against her.

Until this recent threat.

She'd ordered her security team to hide the truth from Gideon, to make the threat seem less severe. She'd almost died because of it. And put their daughters in the crossfire.

Gideon had made sure all three of his daughters, along with Maggie's husband and Tirith's beau, had been sent to secure locations as a precaution. He felt reasonably secure that his daughters would be safe. After all, the letters and emails had threatened Alessandra directly. Not his family.

Now it was up to him to keep Alessandra alive.

"I'm going to walk the perimeter. Then I'll bring in your bags."

He didn't expect a response, and none came.

Exhaustion buffeted him as he stepped outside into the darkness. The sky was littered with stars. No moon out tonight.

He leaned one arm against the side of the house, sagged against the wall, letting it take his weight. His side ached. He wanted to sleep.

Focus.

He had to keep going. This had been *his* plan. Isolate Alessandra until his team, not hers, had neutralized the threat.

It had been a long time since he'd been a Navy SEAL, but he still had connections with that world. He only hoped they would be enough.

He walked the perimeter of the cabin, eyes alert for

any sign that someone had been here recently. Everything was dark and quiet.

At the SUV, he pulled out Alessandra's duffel bag and one of the brown grocery bags. His side protested.

He needed to check the wound. He'd only had time for the doctor to put in a few stitches and toss some antibiotics in his duffel. It had been twelve hours since then.

Inside, Alessandra wasn't immediately visible, and his pulse skyrocketed.

There.

Maybe the bathroom door didn't latch or something because it stood open a couple of inches. He caught sight of her blonde tresses, saw her face pressed into her hands, shoulders trembling.

His first instinct was to go to her. It was a visceral tug, the desire to pull her into his arms, reassure her, comfort her.

Except he wasn't the right guy for the job. Not anymore.

He dropped the bag of groceries on the counter with a thud. "Everything is clear outside."

He crossed to the bed and put her designer leather bag on the end of it. He'd need to scrounge up sheets and a blanket. A chest under the window seemed the likely place for them.

He was bone tired and didn't want to add one more thing to his to-do list, but there was nothing for it. Alessandra didn't need to sleep on a bare mattress.

He was propping the the lid of the chest open when he felt a trickle of warm liquid trail down his side, underneath his T-shirt and the flannel shirt he'd thrown over it.

He bit back a curse word. He needed to be at full speed, full strength. His wound would slow him down if he didn't take care of it.

When Alessandra left the bathroom, he set the sheets and blanket on the end of the bed and went into the bathroom himself.

Pain flared as he took off his shirt.

This was bad.

Alessandra couldn't seem to get warm.

Gideon had noticed on the drive up. He'd turned on the heater and the heated seats.

Gideon noticed everything.

She hated that about him.

She didn't want to be here. To be sequestered with her husband. For him to find out the secret she'd been keeping all these years.

She'd argued for a different solution, but after the attack at Maggie's charity ball, Gideon and Eloise's security team had overruled her.

"It's only a few days." She barely breathed the words, but it was so quiet here—completely silent, unlike the constant bustle in the Glorvaird palace or the steady stream of cowhands at the Triple H—that her whisper sounded as loud as a shout.

"You say something?" Gideon spoke through the cracked bathroom door—the thing had a faulty latch.

She took her cell phone out of her pocket. She hadn't turned it on since yesterday, at Gideon's demand. If she powered it up now, she could guess that there would be no bars. No service.

"Is there wifi?"

She knew the answer before he said it. A remote place like this, more than an hour from the nearest town.

"No." His voice commanding, even with the partly closed door between them. "Keep your cell phone off."

She knew why. Location services could be hacked. But it still rankled to hear him order her around.

"I have the meeting with Ambassador Cain in a week," she said. "There are documents I need to read through. Send changes back through my assistant, Clara."

"You can mark up the paper copy your aide sent." He was maddeningly calm.

There was a rustle of clothing. And that was it. Just mark up the paper copy.

Her temper sparked. "I can't be out of communication for an undetermined period of time. There are people I need to talk to."

He didn't answer. She looked toward the bathroom, imagining banging on the door until he responded to her—

Then she realized he was shirtless.

It was so unexpected that she lost her composure for the briefest moment.

And he was staring at her, dark eyes unreadable.

"Who?" he asked. His voice held a dangerous undertone.

Who, what?

Afraid he would see her icy mask slipping, she shook her head and turned away.

But that didn't stop her brain from fixating on the memory image of him. Gideon wasn't the kind of rancher who sat behind a desk and ordered his cowboys around. He never had been.

And his years of work showed, even on a fifty-something year old body.

She hadn't aged as well as he had. She'd gone soft in

some places, especially after Bea's birth twenty-four years ago.

Gideon didn't have an ounce of softness on him.

She closed her eyes, willing away the image of his broad shoulders and the ropes of muscles down his abdomen.

It didn't help.

What had they been talking about? Communications. Or the lack thereof.

"I need to be able to communicate with Eloise. And Clara. And there are others." She opened her eyes to a wavy reflection of him in the outdated stainless steel fridge.

He remained in the doorway, one arm propped on his hip.

Not on his hip, she realized.

Her surprise had her reacting before she'd thought it through. She whirled and took two steps toward him before her thoughts caught up. She stopped short.

"You're hurt."

Blood, stark red, was soaking through the wad of tissues he held against his left side.

She caught the flash of surprise in his eyes before his expression went carefully blank.

"I got nicked. I'm fine."

She'd seen his nicks before. Once at the ranch, he'd

nearly sliced his finger off while filing a horse's hoof. He'd declared it so minor he didn't need to see a doctor.

She'd overruled him.

But back then, everything had been different. That was before their marriage had transformed into this cold, barren wasteland full of pressure mines.

They stared at each other, all of it hanging almost palpably in the air between them. The words they'd spoken and the ones they hadn't. The missed anniversaries. Their daughters growing up without him. Both of them missing Maggie so deeply for so long.

He looked away first, a muscle jumping in his cheek.

He didn't like this either, she realized. He didn't want to be here with her.

Why had he insisted so furiously, then?

His sense of duty.

Of course.

Like recognized like. She understood duty. She was good at it.

It was everything else that she could never seem to manage.

"The mirror is too high." It seemed as if he was speaking through gritted teeth. "I can't get a good look at it." He twisted and she saw dark stitches against his skin. "Would you... please... take a look for me?"

She had to clear her throat to push words past the lump that wanted to choke her. "Yes. Of course."

Her feet took her to him before she could truly steel herself. The bathroom was minuscule, so she stayed in the doorway and bent to examine his wound.

"Was it...?" She couldn't say the words.

"A bullet. Just grazed me. Doctor checked it out and it passed right through. I'm fine."

He sounded so matter-of-fact, but all she could do was remember how they'd stood together at Maggie's charity ball. One moment, he'd been at a polite distance. Not so far that anyone would know they were estranged. He had once found it difficult to be more a few inches from her. He'd often stayed glued to her side, his hand at her back.

There'd been a crack that split the air, and she'd found herself unceremoniously pushed to the ground. Gideon had covered her body with his.

Was that the moment he'd taken this bullet? One meant for her?

"I just need to know if the stitches held." His voice had gentled.

Had he guessed that her thoughts would spiral in terrible circles?

She breathed in deeply and was shocked by the familiar scent of his skin. He'd used that same soap since she'd met him. She just hadn't been close enough to smell it in ages.

Suddenly uncomfortable, she straightened. "The stitches look all right. But I'm not a doctor."

He nodded, meeting her eyes in the small rectangular mirror that was shoulder-height for his tall frame. "Can you stick a bandage on for me?"

She glanced past him to the sink, where he'd carefully laid out a white gauze square. It had tape on all four sides. All she needed to do was press it over his wound.

She reached past him to pick up the gauze. Her hand brushed his bare arm and the shock of the inadvertent touch sent her eyes flying to his in the mirror.

His gaze was hooded, telling her nothing.

Maybe she was the only one unmanned by the graze of skin against skin.

She grabbed the bandage and carefully lined it up before she pressed it against his skin. This time she was better prepared for the sparks that coursed through her.

"Good enough?" she forced a cool tone into her voice and when he nodded—she couldn't quite meet his eyes now—she turned to retreat.

There was nowhere to run, so she began making up the bed.

It had been a long time since she'd touched a man.

That's what she told herself as she kept her eyes on her task. That was the reason for her overblown reaction. She missed touching, being touched.

It didn't mean anything.

And she needed to get ahold of herself if she was going to keep him from discovering her secret.

Chapter Two

Alessandra opened her eyes. She didn't know how much time had passed or whether she'd dozed off or not.

She rolled over.

The sheets on the bed at this remote cabin weren't the same quality she was used to. The feel of them against her legs was just a shade off uncomfortable.

Or maybe it was the company making her so restless.

There was Gideon, standing where she'd last seen him. He had one shoulder propped against the wall and stared out a sliver of exposed window.

She sighed softly. And she knew he heard, because his eyes flickered briefly.

"It's the middle of the night," she whispered. "You need to sleep."

"I'm fine."

His stitches had just barely opened. He hadn't lost much blood, but a gunshot wound was a gunshot wound. And they'd driven sixteen hours straight to get here.

She had a sudden urge to growl, like some kind of wild animal. Or chuck a pillow at him.

The man was so stubborn. So stubborn.

Well, so was she. Years ago, she had single-handedly convinced the royal council to uphold one of Eloise's only edicts.

She sat up in bed, the sheets folding around her bent knees. Her hair was loose and fell over one shoulder.

"You're not a machine," she argued softly. "You need rest just the same as I do."

Saying the words aloud was a good reminder for her, too. She'd lived in survival mode for so long. Sometimes it was easier to think of Gideon as a machine. A thing with no feelings.

Because if he was a machine, he couldn't mean to hurt her.

Alessandra hated that what had once been a warm relationship, one she'd been sure she couldn't live without, had faded into the same kind of sham marriage as her parents had.

Now he grunted, shifting a little on his feet. Was he in pain?

"I didn't pack a sleeping bag," he said.

Confusion pinched her brow.

Maybe he had 20/20 peripheral vision, because he continued as if she'd spoken her confusion. "There's only one bed."

Oh.

Did it bother him to think about lying in the same bed with her? Heat crept into her cheeks. She turned her face to the side.

"We shared a bed for years," she said. Was that her voice? Husky and soft? "It doesn't bother me."

He was silent and motionless for a moment that stretched long. The longer it stretched, the more she wondered if he was finally going to say all the things that were broken between them.

But then he was a blur in the darkness, taking the two steps from the window to the bed. He sat down gingerly on the edge. He must be in more pain than she'd guessed.

He moved his legs. She heard his shoes thunk onto the floor.

She stretched out again, lying on her back, scooting

away to give him room. It wasn't enough. His shoulder still brushed hers, and she felt the awareness of his touch skitter down her spine.

He was lying on top of the covers. Still fully dressed.

But at least he'd relented. Maybe he would even get some sleep.

She stared at the ceiling, feeling more wide awake now than when they'd arrived.

The hours together had opened her eyes, made her remember that Gideon was tough, a product of his upbringing and his time as a SEAL and the nature of his profession.

He was a man, but he was human. He bled. He hurt.

And he kept that part of himself from her.

Who had started the rift, years ago? The memories were fuzzy now, nebulous. They could blow away if she breathed too heavily.

Thirty years ago, she'd pledged her life to Gideon. She'd trusted him. She'd loved him—and she still did. That was the secret she held so close. Because it was one-sided. And it made her weak.

"Where did we go wrong?" Had she meant to say the words? She'd held them close to her heart for such a long time. Afraid of the answer. Afraid that if she asked, everything would become final. There would be no coming back.

He made a noise halfway between a grunt and a sigh. "I thought you wanted to sleep."

She did. But now that she'd dared to speak the words, she also wanted to know. The question was out there, waiting to be answered.

But he remained silent, and she'd used up all her reserves of bravery for the moment.

Gideon could be reasonable, she reminded herself. She'd fought against this plan, the isolation. But fighting against him hadn't gotten her anywhere. If he was her only chance of ensuring the trade agreement reached Ambassador Cain, she'd make nice.

"This agreement is vitally important," she said softly.

"I know." There was some resignation behind his words, something she didn't understand.

"I have to be back in Glorvaird by next Friday."

It gave her a little more than a week to somehow get her changes on the document to Clara. And the flight would take a whole day.

"Your safety is my priority," he said.

She turned her head slightly toward him. He moved, and they were looking at each other from only inches away. For one breathless moment, she thought about crossing the small space. She missed his kisses. Desperately.

"If you have to miss the press conference with the ambassador, is there someone who can speak in your place?" he asked.

She didn't want to think about that, but sighed and tipped her chin toward the ceiling, breaking eye contact. "I suppose Ronald Arnault is the one who knows most about it."

Gideon was lying still, but somehow when she spoke Ronald's name, he froze. Was he even breathing?

"We'll talk about it tomorrow." He spoke the words with finality and rolled over onto his side, facing away from her.

What had just happened? For a fraction of a moment, she'd thought that maybe he would soften toward her. Maybe they would have a chance to clear the air.

But her timing was off, as usual. He must be exhausted. He was injured.

And she was suddenly buried under the weight of all of it. Trying to keep up her facade. She had never used to hide her true self from Gideon. But there was such a chasm between them.

She would prove she could hold her own during this

perilous time. She wasn't helpless like she had been when they first met.

And she had a duty. A job to complete for the crown. She wouldn't shirk her responsibility.

Gideon was reasonable. She held on to the reminder tightly. They could work together.

Where did we go wrong?

Alessandra's words echoed through Gideon's mind even after she'd fallen asleep.

Her head had turned toward him on the pillow and her even breaths sent warm air across the bare skin of his neck.

All of this was wrong.

He knew that's not what she'd been asking, but he couldn't help thinking it.

It should never have come to gunshots in a crowded ballroom.

If he'd lived in the Glorvaird palace with his wife, he would have known the seriousness of this threat. She wouldn't have been able to hide it from him.

It was thoughts of the other things she wouldn't be able to keep hidden that had kept him from her side all these years.

Ronald Arnault.

Gideon had known the other man would be trouble the moment they'd met in one of the many palace meeting rooms. He should've listened to his gut. He should've been there when his wife needed him.

Not that she would've asked. Ten years after their marriage, the Triple H had experienced a span of difficult years. A country-wide drought, a larger-than-usual loss of cattle to sickness, and Carrie's husband, Trey, had gone through treatments for cancer.

Gideon had come back to Texas, even knowing that Alessandra was tied to Glorvaird, to her duties to the crown. And that's when everything had gone wrong.

How he hated that word. Duty.

If it weren't for his duty to the family ranch and legacy...

If Alessandra had a few less responsibilities...

What had once been a happy, if busy, marriage hadn't survived their individual lives tearing them apart.

And Arnault had been there to pull the pin on the grenade that blew everything up.

He'd never told her he knew. Was too humiliated. Gideon should've been enough for his wife.

Where did we go wrong?

Gideon shouldn't have come out here with her, alone.

He'd kept his hurt to himself for a decade now, along with the knowledge that she'd been having an affair. That Arnault was the one making her laugh and buying her flowers.

Just thinking about it made him want to howl. He clenched his teeth against the desire to make any noise.

Alessandra was his.

That kind of caveman mentality wasn't something Alessandra would appreciate. He'd always kept that side of himself hidden—the greedy, selfish side that wanted her all to himself.

After all these years, he was sure she didn't want to see it now.

He should call in reinforcements. Or take Alessandra to the nearest airport and put her on a plane straight back to Glorvaird and the palace that was built like a fortress.

But this whole thing had been his plan. Keep Alessandra hidden away until time to meet with the Ambassador. Give the FBI team back in Texas long enough to track down the assassins that had attacked during the ball.

His plan to hide Alessandra away was the opposite of her usual modus operandi. Her every move was published by the crown, she took every photo opp. Eloise had relied on her to be the face of the royal family for decades. Everyone in the kingdom, and even on an international level, loved Alessandra.

Gideon loved her, too.

He'd never stopped.

And maybe that was clouding his judgment now. Lord knows, he'd failed Maggie when she'd been twelve and needed him most.

No.

He couldn't think like that.

He turned his head slightly. The moon had come up in the hours since he'd walked the perimeter and light filtered through the blinds he'd closed. It was enough to see her expression relaxed in sleep.

She looked ten years younger.

He'd known her in her twenties, and she was even more beautiful now than she'd been then.

Her lashes formed dark fans against her cheeks. Her mouth was slightly open, and he forced his eyes away from her kissable lips.

He never got to see her like this. Relaxed. At peace.

When they were in a room together, she was always hiding behind a polite, distant mask.

He did it, too.

With every secret they held between them, taking off those masks was too painful.

Stop staring. He pointed his chin up to the ceiling again.

She doesn't want you.

He wasn't going to change the plan now. Not when they'd found safety in this remote cabin. He'd made sure they weren't followed. He'd turned off both cell phones and secured them in a Faraday bag in the back of the SUV after she'd patched him up.

Alessandra was safe.

It was his peace of mind that was in jeopardy.

How long could he stay in this tiny cabin, locked away with the woman he loved—who didn't love him back anymore—and keep his distance?

He'd thought being separated from Alessandra was the hardest thing he'd been through.

This was worse.

Now she was close enough to touch, but she still wasn't for him.

He had to get through this. Keep her alive. Keep his emotions to himself.

Deliver her back home.

Do the job.

Chapter Three

Gideon woke disoriented.

His pillow smelled like Alessandra and in the hazy, half-awake place, he only knew that he ached for her. He reached out and his hand encountered only cool, empty blankets.

Instantly, he came awake. Everything snapped into place in his brain.

His wife.

The danger.

The cabin.

He sat up, rubbing one hand down his face. He ached, but it was the physical pain in his side, not the fanciful imagining his sleep-addled brain wanted him to believe.

Something was sizzling quietly, and he shook his head, still trying to clear his thoughts.

Alessandra stood at the stove, a rubber spatula in hand. She was watching him over her shoulder. He read the concern in her face.

"Are you all right?"

He cleared his own expression, just in case any lingering pain might be visible. "I'm fine."

He was always fine. The bitter thought was quickly shoved away.

He stood up and pretended he wasn't staggering those few steps past the cast iron, pot-bellied fireplace to the bathroom. He'd grown older when he wasn't paying attention. He couldn't go days without sleep. Not anymore. His body was fit for his age, but he wasn't kidding himself that he could go up against a twenty-five-year-old without risking injury.

His most important weapon now was his brain. And he intended to use it.

He splashed his face with icy water and rubbed his skin briskly with the rough hand towel. His side pulled, but he ignored it. He'd pop an ibuprofen along with the antibiotic the doctor had prescribed. He could handle this.

When he re-entered the main room and caught sight of Alessandra scraping scrambled eggs onto two plates, he almost turned around to duck back into the tiny bathroom.

Seeing his royal wife doing such a domestic chore brought him right back to those early days, when she'd found herself sequestered on the Triple H with a bunkhouse full of rowdy cowboys. She was as bad with inaction as Gideon. She'd cleaned the ranch house top to bottom. Cooked for them. Made the house a home.

The ranch house still bore some of her touches, but nothing was the same without her there.

He pushed those thoughts away as he joined her at the counter, reaching for the chipped coffee mug she pushed toward him.

"Thank you," he gruffed. She'd always called his rough morning voice his bear growl.

Would the hits keep coming this morning?

"You're welcome." She was watching him, her gaze curious. Checking to see if he was really all right?

He raised his mug. She did the same, taking a delicate sip.

His brows crunched together, and he lowered his cup before he'd taken a drink. That wasn't tea in her mug.

"Since when do you drink coffee?"

She lowered her cup, her eyes following the motion

as she set the mug on the counter. "I acquired the taste about five years ago. And there's no kettle."

He hadn't thought to pack one. They'd been in such a rush. He knew he'd put her tea bags in one of the grocery sacks, but he hadn't given a thought as to whether or not there'd be a way to heat up the water.

"Sorry," he muttered. He hid his frown behind a sip of coffee. It was something else he didn't know about his wife. They were practically strangers now, weren't they? Even with three grown daughters between them.

The coffee turned bitter in his throat.

He scarfed down the eggs and toast she'd made, earning himself a sideways look that viscerally reminded him of their first meeting.

Then he took his meds. Started pulling on his boots.

"Are you going for firewood?" she asked. "It feels colder in here today."

He glanced around at the threadbare furnishings. There was no more wood in the iron holder near the stove. "Older cabins like this aren't always insulated that well. I'll grab some wood after I do some reconnaissance."

A haughty, bossy expression came over her. "What does that mean?"

He opened the door to find a light snow falling.

"I'm going to take a look around. Maybe hike down

toward the road and make sure nobody's been in the woods since last night."

Her frown turned fierce. "It's snowing."

I know. He didn't say the words.

"And you're injured."

He grabbed the black vest from the small pile of belongings. "I'm fine. I'm hale enough to keep you safe. Let me do my job."

Her mouth trembled before she firmed her lips, a hardness overtaking her expression. Somehow he'd said the wrong thing.

He shrugged into the vest, ignoring the pull in his side. "I might be gone an hour. There's a second pistol locked in the case. There."

He pointed to a high shelf on the wall where he'd stashed his backup weapon. He'd given Alessandra shooting lessons himself, but that'd been years ago. He didn't know whether she'd kept up the practice. He didn't ask.

"I'll bring in some firewood when I come back."

He'd seen a pile stacked neatly between two trees, last night when he'd walked the perimeter of the cabin. It was set off from the cabin, at the edge of the woods.

He ducked outside without waiting for her to speak.

Last night, he'd been sure he could handle this. But being faced with a wife who had cooked breakfast, taken care of him? Not to mention how incredibly beautiful she was with her hair loose and a too-big sweatshirt.

For a long time, he'd been the only one who'd seen the softer, private side of the princess. The woman she could be at home, not the public face she showed when necessary.

He grumbled under his breath as he hiked away from the cabin. He needed to find his equilibrium.

He didn't walk a straight path through the pine forest that surrounded the cabin. For one thing, the mountainside grew steeper and steeper, and he had to take a roundabout path to keep from sliding down on his tookus. He also wanted the chance to catch any footprints or broken twigs, and he didn't know which direction an enemy might've come from.

It took longer than he'd thought to reach the winding mountain road they'd driven up yesterday. The air seemed to grow colder as he followed the road in both directions, from far enough away that he remained mostly hidden in the trees.

He didn't see any signs that anyone had been there.

That was good.

What wasn't good? His extremities numb from cold. It was well into spring back home in Texas. He hadn't packed winter gloves or thick wool socks. He hadn't been prepared for a spring mountain snowstorm.

His fault.

His side burned with every step now. Had he over-done it?

He stopped to lean against a long-dead tree. Its lower branches were gone, and some animal had stripped the bark from the trunk. At least it still held his weight as he tried to catch his breath.

He couldn't see the cabin through the snow, falling more thickly now. He'd thought he'd be back by now. Had he gotten turned around?

Was Alessandra still cold in the cabin? Had she packed better than he had? Did she have warm clothes to bundle up in?

His brain was getting sluggish. That was the real danger.

He forced himself to keep moving. If he died out here, who would keep Alessandra alive?

Something big hit the side of the cabin.

Alessandra jumped, several pages of papers she'd spread across the counter floating to the floor.

What was that?

Heart racing, she stood on trembling legs.

More than an hour had passed since Gideon had gone out. Closer to two.

Then a sound like scratching against the outside of the wall. On the north side. Where there were no windows. The door was on the west wall.

Was it an animal? A bear, able to smell the food she'd cooked earlier? She'd read news stories of bear attacks.

She glanced at the metallic case on the high shelf Gideon had motioned to earlier.

She had some training, but she was nervous to even hold a gun.

What should she—?

A moan, louder than the wind that had been rattling the windowpanes.

She strained her ears to hear over the pulse pounding through her head. More rustling.

"Allie."

That was Gideon. She was sure of it. Sure enough to go to the door and pull it open, though she kept her body hidden behind the wooden panel.

"Gideon?" she called.

If it wasn't her husband, he was going to be angry with her.

"Allie. Help."

That was his voice, for sure.

She'd slipped into her shoes earlier, more because her feet were cold than any notion of going outside. She didn't bother with a coat now, just rushed out into the biting wind. Big, fluffy snowflakes landed on her hair and the exposed skin of her neck and hands.

He was leaning heavily on the house as he rounded the corner, moving slowly toward her.

"Gideon!" She went to him without a second thought, her arm going around his waist to support him.

His vest was covered in a thin layer of snow, his hand a block of ice when he grabbed onto her shoulder to steady himself.

"Why aren't you wearing gloves?" It was a silly thing to ask, but it was the first thing her mind latched onto.

"D-didn't h-have any," he mumbled through chattering teeth.

"Come on," she urged. "We have to get you inside."

It was only a few steps, but with his weight heavy against her and his feet dragging, the door seemed so far away.

One step. Two.

He stumbled. Even with her feet braced apart, they both almost went down.

She cried out. He gasped. Was he in pain? Was it his injury?

"You make me so angry," she cried out as she made a huge lunge toward the door.

He caught himself on the door frame, keeping them both from falling. Somehow, they shouldered him inside.

She was panting now, sweating a little beneath her layers from the exertion.

"You aren't thirty anymore," she said quietly, angrily. Tears were gathering in her throat and that made her angry too. "You can't just hare off into the woods. What if you'd frozen to death out there?"

His eyes were half-closed, his teeth chattering. He didn't answer.

He could be suffering from hypothermia. Her brain started to whirl in useless circles. She didn't know what to do. She couldn't get on her phone to find answers.

Get him warm.

That's all she could think.

New anger rose, anger that she hadn't gone out to find the woodpile herself. The small heater wasn't keeping up with the temperature outside, though it was warmer in here than out in the elements.

She needed to get him dry. Then she could build a fire in the pot-bellied stove in one corner of the cabin.

He hadn't moved since they'd come inside, only

remained leaning against the wall. Was he even coherent?

"Come on," she demanded. "You need dry clothes." She reached up to unzip the vest and push it off his shoulders.

He gave a mumbled protest when she dragged his shirt over his head, grunted in pain when she made him raise his left arm. His bandage was still in place. She'd need to check it, but not now.

She went for the blanket from the bed as he struggled out of his pants.

"Get in the bed." She threw the blanket over his shoulders, but he seemed disoriented and didn't move.

She thought of giving him a little shove, but worried about his wound.

When she tugged him by the hand, he followed her the few steps to the bed, more docile than she'd ever known him to be. When she tried to step away so he could lie down, he wouldn't let go of her. He kept hold of her hand, pulling her close until she was tangled up in the blanket with him.

"Gideon!"

Maybe he fell or maybe it was intentional, but he took her onto the bed with him. He was behind her, snuggling like two spoons. He nuzzled his face into her hair.

"You're warm," he mumbled.

This wasn't a real embrace. He was only trying to get warm. And they'd both be embarrassed when he came to his senses and realized how he was holding her.

But she didn't tell him to let go. Didn't roll away.

One of his hands gripped the blanket, just in front of her midsection. She covered his icy hand with both of hers, settling there. Trying to share her warmth with him.

He didn't move, didn't speak for long minutes. He shifted slightly, and only then did she realize she'd relaxed against him.

"I'm sorry," he whispered into her hair. His teeth were still chattering, his words slightly slurred.

"You should be," she whispered back. "I didn't think you were coming back."

Just the thought of it now set a spiral of anxiety loose in her stomach.

"I lost your trust." His words slurred. "I saw it happening, and I couldn't stop it."

She tried to turn her head to see him, but his arm was heavy, trapping her where she was. Was he talking about today? It sounded as if he was having a whole other conversation.

"Gideon—"

"I tried to find Maggie, but I couldn't."

A shudder shook him.

Maggie? Find Maggie? Was he talking about the kidnapping?

Those had been dark days. Alessandra had been so worried about the twins, and she'd taken out her fear and anger on Gideon, even though he didn't deserve it.

"Maggie is fine," she whispered. "She's at the safe house with Luc. Tirith and Bea are safe too."

He rolled his head, the movement anxious. "I should've found her. I should've been the one."

Did he really believe that? The palace had invoked emergency help from every agency available to them. The police, the palace guard, international law enforcement, private investigators.

A local Glorvaird policeman had found Maggie at last.

"You did everything you could," she whispered.

It was my fault.

Those words she kept inside. Maggie and Tirith had been at an event Alessandra had planned. The palace security team had made mistakes, yes, but it was Alessandra's event. She didn't dare ask forgiveness from Gideon, not when she couldn't forgive herself.

A soft snore startled her. How long had she been lost in the past?

Was it dangerous for him to sleep?

She slowly ran her hand up his arm. His skin seemed to be warming. Would he be all right?

Even in his sleep, his arms tightened around her.

"Don't see Arnault again," he demanded in a sleepy voice. "I hate him."

"Gideon—"

Another snore. Was he talking in his sleep?

Why would he say such a thing? Ronald was a close member of her team. He was instrumental in the work Alessandra did for the crown. He'd become a friend over the past decade.

Maybe Gideon was dreaming about something else.

Though she was still worried about him, she slipped from his embrace, throwing a glance over her shoulder to ensure he was still sleeping.

She put on an extra sweatshirt and went out into the snow. She had to find that firewood.

Chapter Four

Gideon came to when the door quietly closed. Unlike earlier—or was it yesterday?—there was no disorientation.

The bathroom door was open, the light off.

Where was Alessandra? Had she gone outside?

He sat up in the bed, and as the blanket fell away, he realized he was mostly undressed. He remembered being out in the snowstorm, losing track of time and direction, but his memories of reaching the cabin were fuzzy and full of holes.

He'd been glad to see Alessandra. So glad. He'd wanted to grab her and kiss her.

He'd been clumsy, falling against the cabin to stay upright.

Now every muscle hurt. His skin hurt.

He staggered to the window and pushed back the blind. Relief surged when he saw Alessandra, her hair like a flag behind her, heading for the wood pile.

The snow had stopped, and the wood pile wasn't far, but it was growing dark, and shadows cast by the trees around them had an ominous feel.

She shouldn't be out there alone.

Had he slept the day away?

So much for being a heroic protector.

Worry sent him to his duffel. A minor bout of dizziness slowed him down, but he managed to get a pair of jeans on. He was pulling a T-shirt over his head when the door opened and sent a blast of chilled air across his bare feet.

Alessandra came inside, arms full of wood.

"You're up." He heard the same relief in her voice that he'd felt moments ago. Had she been worried about him?

"So I am." He was opening his mouth to apologize that she'd had to light the fire and tend it all day when she turned and knelt next to the pot-bellied stove. Her armful of wood clattered to the floor.

"I was beginning to think I was going to have to drive down the mountain in the dark on icy roads."

He frowned. Alessandra rarely drove herself anywhere—or she hadn't back when they'd been close.

She always had a driver or a security guard behind the wheel. Why—?

"To take you to a hospital." She tossed the words over her shoulder, and he caught the glint of unshed tears in her eyes before she gave him her back.

His heart in his throat, he took a step closer.

She didn't seem to register his motion. She opened the stove door with a creak and fed in two chunks of split wood. She closed the door but remained where she was, kneeling on the floor with her shoulders hunched.

He couldn't help himself. He crossed the space between them and reached out to touch her shoulder.

"Allie, I'm sorry—"

He wasn't prepared for the hit when he glimpsed her teary eyes, wasn't prepared for her to awkwardly launch herself at him, to knock him on his butt on the floor.

She was in his arms, clinging tightly to him, and he didn't care that she'd swept him off his feet.

He held her as she breathed into the neck of his shirt. She wasn't crying, not that he could tell. She'd always been tough.

He should let her go, get her a tissue or something. But instead, he found himself rubbing her back in soothing strokes. Every moment he held her heightened the storm inside of him. He'd missed this. Missed her. A constant pain. As if a part of him was missing.

"I'm sorry I scared you," he murmured into her hair.

She drew in a shuddery breath and then her head tipped back, giving him a close up view of the concern in her wet eyes.

"Are you in pain? How much pain are you in?" She corrected herself. "And don't say I'm fine."

He couldn't help the curve of his lips at her petulant demand. He brushed one long strand of her hair behind her ear. "I don't hurt anywhere."

It was true. Even the throbbing of his wound had dulled. Give him a full night's rest and he'd be back at full speed.

Her gaze skimmed his face. What was she looking for? He was telling the truth.

Suddenly, she was leaning toward him. Her mouth brushed his and all thought fled.

Alessandra was kissing him.

And it was glorious. Like coming home. Like fireworks on a Fourth of July. Like perfection.

One of her hands threaded into the hair at his nape.

His hands curled around her waist. He couldn't get enough of her. His wife. His.

The primal thought broke through. He gentled his mouth and then pulled away from the kiss.

She wasn't his. Not anymore.

What were they doing? When she walked away from him in a few days, it was going to decimate his heart. Again.

But he still couldn't quite make himself let her go completely. He pressed his jaw against her temple as she panted, trying to catch her breath.

We probably shouldn't have done that. He bit back the words that would only hurt them both.

"I'm sorry I scared you," he said again.

She drew away. He let her go.

Though they were sitting a foot apart on the floor in front of the stove, his arms felt empty. His soul felt empty.

"Maybe we shouldn't have come here alone."

Her words battered him. If he'd planned better, if he'd had a team instead of stubbornly insisting it be only him...

"Maybe you're right."

He hadn't been enough to rescue Maggie. The thought slipped into his consciousness. A memory, a hazy one, of being half-frozen and holding Alessandra. He'd said *I should've found her. I should've been the one.*

This was the true cost of his stubbornness, insisting that isolation was the only way. There was nowhere to hide when the painful past they shared jumped out in the open between them.

It had happened so long ago. But the pain was still there, eating him up. That pain felt new again, slicing him open inside. Making him bleed. Was it the same for her? She didn't deserve that. Maybe being here was a chance for them to get this out in the open.

"When Maggie got grabbed—"

Her soft gasp interrupted him.

His hand crossed the chasm between them, curled around hers. And she let him.

"I tried to find her. I thought I was close but—" He shook his head. He'd found nothing. An abandoned warehouse that had been a dead end. No connection to the actual kidnapper.

She squeezed his hand, bringing him out of that terrifying place he'd gone to in his mind.

"That wasn't your job. Not yours alone," she said when he opened his mouth to protest. "You were a frightened father."

He'd been terrified. He knew what evil men could do, had seen it firsthand during his time with the SEALs. Maggie had been helpless.

"I should've seen something. Done more."

She let go of him, and he felt the loss of her touch

keenly. She turned her face away, but not before he saw a silver tear slip down her cheek.

"It wasn't your fault. It was mine." Her voice was choked. "I'm the reason Maggie was taken."

* * *

Alessandra wasn't touching Gideon, but she felt him go dangerously still.

"How do you figure that?"

Her husband was one of the smartest men she knew. Maybe he wanted her to spell it out for him.

"The girls were in attendance at that event at my request." Putting it into words was painful. She couldn't look at him, so she tilted her face to one side.

"That wasn't your fault."

"Of course it was."

"How could you have known the girls would be targeted?"

Gideon wasn't a cruel man. She couldn't understand why he was playing dumb. She didn't expect forgiveness or absolution—but she hadn't expected him to make her say it aloud like this.

She inhaled and exhaled, her breath shaky. She was trying to make her words less so.

She couldn't stop another tear, then another, from

slipping down her cheeks. She brushed them away quickly.

"Allie—"

Gideon sounded strangled.

She wished he would stop calling her that. He hadn't addressed her so informally in years. It reminded her of nights spent in the ranch house bed, in a house that'd been in Gideon's family for generations. Gideon had liked to sleep with her tucked right up against him, his arm a warm weight around her. He'd whisper, "G'night, Allie," right before he fell asleep.

Now, it just hurt.

She wiped her face again, still unable to look at him. "We both know I'm to blame. That's why you pulled away." It was the only reason that made sense, all these years later.

"What?" His voice was flat, still with that dangerous undertone.

She glanced at him and then away. "You stayed away."

"Maggie needed me." There was a softening, a resignation to his voice when he said their daughter's name. And then a coolness slipped through. "And you didn't."

The words were an unexpected blow, one that rattled her, stole her breath.

"Of course, I needed you."

When he didn't reply, she glanced at him. He had turned his cheek so he was in profile to her. A muscle jumped in his jaw and his brows were drawn like a thundercloud.

He shook his head slightly. "I can't do this." He stood up, grimacing.

Was it his gunshot wound? Was he in pain?

She stood up too, desire warring within her. She wanted to touch him again, feel for herself that he was alive and well. But there was also fear. He was putting distance between them again. It felt safer to leave it be.

But was it safe to feel alone all the time? To miss him so deeply that she sometimes couldn't eat? Couldn't sleep?

"What can't you do?" she demanded.

His eyes flashed at her before he turned away. "That ice princess bit doesn't work on me. Never has."

"Gideon, don't walk away from me. From this." She dared to reach out and stop him with a hand on his arm. Beneath her touch, he was tense. "Why do you think I didn't need you?"

"Because you had him. Arnault." Another man might've spoken the words explosively. But Gideon had never shouted. When he was most angry, he got quiet.

She felt the reverberation of his near-whispered

words, as if they'd been a bomb detonating between them.

Her hand fell away from his arm.

"Ronald?" Her own anger spiked. "Please tell me you don't believe the drivel those gossip rags write."

"It isn't what they write," he said bitterly. "It's how Arnault looks at you in the photos. Like a sappy, love-struck fool."

She felt as if he'd slapped her.

"I have never been unfaithful to you." The words trembled, like her body, from the force of her anger. "Is this really what's kept us apart all these years? Paparazzi photos? You should've just asked me—"

"I didn't need to." Now he exploded, a little, one hand flying out from his side.

She flinched. He ran his hand through his hair.

"I flew to Glorvaird for your birthday." He exhaled, a bitter sound. "It was supposed to be a surprise. You can't imagine how difficult it was to leave Maggie. She was still so vulnerable. She'd only started speaking again." He paced to the window and stared out. "I bypassed everybody in the palace, coming to see you. And when I arrived at your private chambers, he was there. You were in this embrace..." He shook his head, as if he could wipe the memory. "I'd seen a few photos of you together. I already knew how he felt about you. But the look on your face..."

He clamped his mouth shut, but she'd heard enough. What he'd seen had devastated him.

How could she fix this? How did she tend a wound so deep and so old?

New tears fell, these for the pain Gideon had gone through, for the years they'd lost.

"I have never been unfaithful to you," she whispered. "I swear it. I gave you my heart. Not anyone else."

"Honey, I saw..." She heard the resignation in his tone.

Shook her head. "I can't even remember what we were working on. A proposal for the royal council, maybe? I'd been terribly distracted. My family was falling apart. I never told Ronald. Eloise was the only one who knew. He worked seventy-two hours straight and rewrote the proposal. Maybe you saw gratefulness on my expression. I was grateful. He saved that proposal when I was too heartbroken to do right for my country." She wiped her face again. "There's only ever been friendship between us."

She wished she would have known. All this time... all the wasted years between them. Maybe they could've been spared some of the pain and loneliness.

He stared at her, and she willed him to see she was

telling the truth. She'd given Gideon her heart. No one else.

He blew out a loud breath, startling her. Rubbed both hands down his face."I don't know what to think right now."

She wanted him to reach for her. To hold her again, kiss her like he had not that long ago.

"By the time I hit the tarmac back in Texas, it was like what had happened was confirmation of what I already knew. Maggie needed me—in Texas. The ranch needed me. And you were tied to Glorvaird." *Still are.*

He didn't say the last part out loud, but she knew he must be thinking it. She had a deadline to get back to. A proposal to finish. Her country needed her. She had a duty.

Thirty years ago, they'd believed they could do it all. She could work for the crown, uphold the family legacy. And Gideon could manage the Triple H with help from Carrie and Trey.

But those parts of their lives had pulled them in opposite directions. Still were.And she didn't know how to change that. Whether or not it could be changed.

She would always be a princess. Glorvaird needed her.

And Gideon would always feel the pull to Texas, running the ranch and the charity.

She ached from wanting to be close to him again, but he didn't cross the space that separated them.

And neither did she.

"Maybe we should get some rest," he offered. "Tonight's been... a lot."

He was right. Of course he was.

But she hated the distance between them as they passed each other, brushing teeth and changing clothes in the bathroom, lying silently in the dark.

She was drifting off to sleep when she came awake with a realization.

He'd never actually said he believed her.

It took her much longer to fall asleep after that.

Chapter Five

"Are you warm enough?"

Alessandra glanced up from watching the sidewalk pass beneath her feet. Gideon was beside her, handsome in jeans and a dark coat over his T-shirt.

She was the only one who knew he'd strapped a shoulder holster beneath his clothing.

"I'm plenty warm." The air chilled her cheeks and neck, but she was bundled up. It was a few minutes before twilight, and the snow had moved off several days ago.

They'd come off the mountain to get supplies, to this quaint, tiny town with a Main Street that reminded her of an American sitcom from the nineteen-fifties. The brick-and-glass buildings were so different from the historical architecture in Glorvaird. And she loved it. There was even a small park ahead, in the town square.

"This way." Gideon guided her with a touch at the small of her back, but she balked at the shadowy indoor stairway between two storefronts.

Gideon was glancing both ways, reading the street around them, and didn't seem to notice.

When he moved forward, she reluctantly went with him. His arm came around her waist, as if they were teenagers who couldn't keep their hands off each other.

"Sorry to be overbearing," he murmured.

"You're not."

Things had been... strange between them these past few days. They hadn't spoken of Ronald again, but there'd been an openness, a hopefulness in the quiet moments spent together in the cabin.

Or maybe that was all on her side.

She didn't think so. Not when she caught the occasional thoughtful glance Gideon directed at her.

She'd been the one caught staring at his lips when she'd been curled up on the tiny sofa, supposed to be reading through the documents for Ambassador Cain. He hadn't kissed her again, but she couldn't stop thinking about his kiss.

At the top of the stairs, Gideon reached past her to

pull open a heavy, metal door. He shielded her with his body momentarily. Then light streamed around them.

A familiar scent hit her. Books. A library.

"Thought maybe you'd want to check your emails."

A part of her was happy to stay in the little bubble they'd lived in for the past four days. Without the outside world pulling her in all directions, she'd been reminded of the quiet protector her husband was. The man who worked tirelessly without expecting thanks.

She hadn't asked for her phone, not after that first day. And a part of her hesitated even now as she stepped inside the public library. Once she opened her emails, the real world would demand her time and attention.

Things would change.

She didn't want the world to intrude. She hadn't found a way to say what she needed to say yet, to clear the air fully with Gideon. Because she couldn't see a way forward.

If she admitted she still loved him... then what? They'd tried and failed to keep their marriage together when they both had duties to attend to on different continents.

But there was no putting it off. She sat down at one of the six public computers. The machine was old and shaped like a box. How long would it take to load a browser-based email program?

Gideon stood nearby, pretending to peruse a shelf of crime thrillers. She knew he was diligently watching.

Not that there was much to be wary of. The librarian had smiled at them from behind her desk near the door when they'd entered. There was maybe one other patron browsing in the stacks at the rear of the building.

Her assistant was worth her weight in gold, for only three emails had been flagged that needed Alessandra's attention. Two she was able to answer immediately. The third was from Eloise, asking for an update. Alessandra closed the browser window and cleared the cache without answering.

She should've finished the proposal by now. She could've found a courier for her handwritten notes on the document. She was letting her sister down—her country down—by mooning over her husband.

She couldn't continue like this.

She stood and went to Gideon. "I'm finished."

He took them a more circuitous way to the door, so that they passed by a bank of windows overlooking main street.

He was so determined to keep her safe.

"This way," he murmured on the street. They walked toward the park, but the SUV was down the street in the other direction. Where—?

She grew distracted as they passed the park entrance. A mother and teenage daughter sat with a picnic blanket, where they'd set up a big cardboard box. On the side of the box in thick, black marker strokes was written "Puppies for sale".

Two floppy ears and a snout covered in blond fur peeked above the edge of the box.

Alessandra glanced at Gideon, only to find him watching her. His eyes had gone soft, and the corner of his mouth was twitching.

"You'd better stop for a minute."

It was all the permission she needed.

"May I?" she asked the mother, who nodded.

She knelt on the blanket and reached inside the box where there were not one, but three puppies.

They were happy for the attention and clambered all over each other to try to get to her. She laughed when one got close enough to lick her chin.

A sneaky glance at Gideon showed he was watching her, smiling. Not keeping an eye on their surroundings at all.

"Did you—?" He couldn't have planned this.

"I saw the sign when we were driving through." Not planned, but he'd brought her down the street just so he could give her this moment.

The man knew her every weakness. Knew she could never resist a puppy.

For a moment, she let herself get caught in his smile, let herself imagine what it would be like to stand up and throw herself into a hug.

He'd catch her.

But she didn't. No one in this town knew who she was, but there was still decorum. When she stood up, she beamed at him. He seemed to steel himself, before he looked away.

Gideon might know everything about her, but he didn't know she was falling in love with him all over again.

"Time to go?" she asked.

He nodded.

They walked on the opposite side of the street this time. As they came out of the park, a teenager and her boyfriend were passing. The girl did a double-take, but then seemed to forget about them as she kept walking with her friend. Gideon had noticed, though he didn't seem bothered.

The setting sun shining off the mountain behind the buildings across the street distracted Alessandra. It was picturesque.

And then Gideon took her hand.

Her face flooded with heat. He didn't seem to notice

as he nodded to the movie theater marquee. They were nearly underneath it.

He didn't wait for her to answer, but ducked inside, pulling her by the hand. The interior was dimly lit and smelled slightly musty—how old was this building?—but she didn't care.

Until he dropped her hand and slipped past her to check the door.

Her smile faded.

She'd thought—

She'd hoped—

Gideon came next to her, pointing toward a hallway that led alongside one wall. A red exit sign glowed.

"What's the matter?"

His low murmur reached her ears as she allowed herself to be hustled in that direction. "Nothing."

He stopped her when someone came out of the theater itself. An employee.

"Not nothing," she said.

He stood close in front of her. Watching her closely.

"I didn't mean to scare you. That girl started video-ing. I couldn't be sure, but it looked like she was pointing her phone at us."

Of course, he'd been paying attention. Protecting her, even when she'd been distracted.

"What's wrong?" He was apparently paying close attention to her now.

"Nothing. It's fine."

He clearly didn't believe her. He waited patiently, his eyes demanding answers.

Embarrassed, she had to look over his shoulder to get the words out. "I thought it was real. That we had come in here to watch a movie."

"Like a date? Would you really want that?"

* * *

Like a date? Would you really want that?

Alessandra's soft but certain, "Yes," twisted Gideon's stomach in a knot.

He checked over his shoulder. The lobby in this single-theater movie house was empty. The uniformed employee had disappeared for now.

Which meant Gideon was free to lean his elbow on the wall Alessandra had scooted next to and lean. Not too far into her personal space, but enough that she would be able to tell he was interested.

She tipped her head back to look into his face. Man, he'd missed her.

"Being with you these few days has been..." She

trailed off and he braced for what might come. Difficult. Strange. Harrowing.

"A blessing." Her voice caught on the words. "I'd forgotten so many things. I've just... missed you."

"Me, too, Princess." He couldn't help himself. He stepped in and scooped her into a hug.

Holding her was the one thing that made sense. She fit in his arms. Her cheek laid right over his heart. She smelled like whatever custom-made shampoo she used and the sweetness that was all her.

He never wanted to let her go.

A commotion came from behind him. Voices.

"I think they came in here."

He had Alessandra moving with a hand at her back before whoever it was made it through the front door.

They ducked down the dark hallway toward what he hoped was a rear exit. Alessandra went tense in the darkness, her breathing hitched.

"I've got you," he whispered.

"Is it—?"

"It's not assassins. Some dumb teenager with a phone must've recognized you."

"If they get a video of you on social and it goes viral..."

He didn't have to finish the sentence. She already

knew. A random small-town teenager could bring down a heap of trouble on them.

He found the exit door with his hand. Prayed it wouldn't set off some kind of alarm as he pushed it open.

It didn't. No lights flashed or siren rang out. Probably the teenagers who worked here used the door to sneak in a friend every now and then.

Out in the alley, he took his bearings. There was a single lane running behind the buildings on this side of main street. No cars parked back here and a clear view to the end of the block on both sides. No foot traffic.

Thank God for small towns.

Alessandra took the gray scarf she'd had wrapped around her neck and tucked her hair up under it, did some magic until it was tied around her head like she was a movie star in an old-fashioned film.

"That ain't gonna work," he commented lightly. "Now everyone's just going to focus on your pretty face."

She rolled her eyes, but he got the blush he was trying for.

She tucked in closer to his side and he let his arm wrap around her shoulder. He wasn't too worried. This alley would put them out right across the street from where he'd parked the SUV.

But if she wanted an excuse to be close to him... well, he wasn't going to complain.

He hustled her into the car, the dark tinted windows a measure of safety, when he spotted the teen girl cruising the street, looking in all directions. The boy she'd been with was trailing behind her, looking miffed.

"Time to vacate this area," he said as he turned on the engine.

Alessandra didn't look up from buckling her seat belt. "Whatever you think."

She was going along without protesting?

"It might be a long ride."

She looked at him, and he felt the force of her gaze in his soul. "Good."

That knot in his gut twisted tighter.

He pulled out into traffic, making his way out of town and back down the mountain. She settled in, curling one leg beneath her and pulling a thick sheaf of papers out of the leather satchel she'd tucked in the floorboard earlier.

They'd both taken precautions and brought all their stuff out of the cabin. Not that they had much.

He snuck glances at her as he drove. She pored over what must be the big proposal she'd been so worried about when they'd first come up the mountain. She tapped her pen on the page. Then scribbled something. Clamped the end of the pen between her teeth.

Every once in awhile, she glanced over at him. The warmth in her eyes hadn't been there on day one.

After almost an hour, she put away her papers, tucked her head against her bent elbow, and drifted off.

She was so beautiful that he had to remind himself to keep his eyes on the road.

He wasn't kidding himself that everything between them was hunky dory now. There were still things that had been left unsaid.

She'd claimed there was nothing between her and Arnault, but Gideon had seen plenty of photos and video of the other man in the same room with Alessandra. Maybe she was innocent, but the man cared about her deeply. Was maybe even in love with her.

And Gideon was supposed to just let her walk back into a committee meeting where she'd sit right next to him? He'd once read an interview where Arnault had disparaged Gideon, though in the most polite terms imaginable. *The Princess's husband was not available for this meeting. He has his own interests overseas.*

Gideon hated the guy.

But Alessandra claimed he was a friend.

He didn't know whether he could be okay with that.

Besides, he had a life in Texas. A family legacy spanning generations. He'd spent the past fifteen years on the ranch building a new herd, growing the infrastructure for the Triple H. He didn't know if he was fit to live in the royal palace anymore.

Or if Alessandra would want that.

Things had changed between them, sure. He wanted his family back. His wife back. But just because she'd warmed up to him a little, would she be happy sitting in a movie theater next to him? That didn't mean she wanted all of it. The good and the bad.

He didn't have any answers by the time he stopped driving.

It was well after dark. The fact that no one had known their destination, except for the palace staff and security he'd notified, meant the tarmac was empty save a security car and the private plane, with its steps extended.

Gideon sighed.

He got out of the car and rounded the front, opened Alessandra's door gently. He didn't want to frighten her.

"Wake up, honey." He brushed the back of her hand with his thumb and she came to with a little sound, half hum and half purr.

She didn't even know where they were, but she smiled at him so beautifully it was like a kick in the gut.

"I like it when you call me honey," she murmured.

She reached for him, and he was very aware that this might be their last moments alone together.

He curled his hand around her jaw and claimed her with his kiss. She met him sweetly, her nose brushing his cheek when she turned her head for a better angle.

He heard a voice from far away. The last thing he needed was for her to be embarrassed. So he pulled away, both of them breathing hard.

I love you. The words remained trapped behind his breastbone. He had the worst timing ever.

She brushed aside her hair that had fallen in her eyes. She seemed alert now, looking to their surroundings.

"Are we—? Gideon, what's going on?"

He gestured to the private plane. "It's time to go home."

Chapter Six

I *don't want to go without you.*

Alessandra had spoken the words before she'd exited the SUV.

At that moment, Gideon's heart had leapt, knocking against his sternum.

But hours later, he was sitting on a fancy leather seat on that private plane staring out the window at the ocean below.

Alone.

He hadn't been surprised in the least when she'd been whisked away by an aide and quickly surrounded by an advisor and a stylist. Two security guys sat near the front of the plane, at ease for the moment.

Gideon had been plied with food and drink by the attendant and left to himself.

They were getting close now. Glorvaird was waiting for Alessandra. She'd slip back into her old life, and he would...?

What had he thought? That by stepping on this plane he was making some big gesture? The threat wasn't over. Someone was out there, possibly even on the ground in Glorvaird by now. Alessandra was determined to proceed with her meeting with Ambassador Cain. Gideon wasn't needed as a bodyguard. And they hadn't made any declarations.

Through the space between two seats, he could see her blonde hair cascading past her shoulders.

If she'd wanted him to stay for her, wouldn't she have spared a few minutes in the hours they'd been on the plane to come and talk to him?

Maybe this was his answer.

He felt the change in altitude before he'd come to any decision. The easiest thing would be to hop on a commercial flight back home. A convoy of security would be waiting for Alessandra on the ground. They wouldn't make the mistake of taking this threat too lightly, not after what'd happened at Maggie's ball.

But just thinking about that made his stomach twist.

The plane touched down. He only had his duffel bag, the strap was quickly thrown over his shoulder.

Alessandra was closer to the door when the release

was turned and the steps extended. He'd been right about the convoy. Through the window, he could see two black SUVs and several men in suits and dark sunglasses standing at attention.

Maybe it would be better to say his goodbyes here, where there was a modicum of privacy.

But by the time he'd gone out into the aisle, Alessandra was being escorted out the door by her security team.

His feet hit the tarmac and he breathed in deeply. How long had it been since he'd stepped foot here? He'd never forgotten the scent of ocean air, the rocky landscape beyond the airport buildings and a high fence.

She glanced over her shoulder and their gazes clashed. There was something in her expression, something vulnerable. Maybe this didn't have to be another end for them.

He followed her off the plane. The sun shone brightly, and he wished he hadn't forgotten his sunglasses in the SUV back in the States.

Alessandra was several paces ahead of him, between the two guards. He was familiar with this private section of the airport. Security was tight and it would be near-impossible for a threat to get through.

Still, he appreciated that the security guys were

hustling her toward the safety of that SUV, with its bullet-proof glass.

Or was she the one hurrying?

Because standing next to the open door of the first SUV was Arnault, in a crisp suit, looking like a million bucks.

Gideon's stomach plunged.

Arnault was her welcoming committee? So much for *there's nothing between us.*

The guy was watching her approach with a starry-eyed expression, and Gideon suddenly couldn't stand it. He wasn't staying.

Couldn't.

He jogged a few steps as her escort came even with a handful of other security guys.

"Alessandra," he called out.

One of the big, bear-like figures stepped into his path and nearly bowled him over.

"Hang on, buddy." The kid couldn't have been older than Bea. He was clean-shaven and bulky-shouldered. Just looking at him made Gideon feel old. "You got a press badge or something? Why don't you give Her Highness a minute—"

Heat flashed into Gideon's face. It'd been years since he'd been mistaken for a commoner—back when he and Alessandra had first married.

"It's all right." Alessandra was right there, flanked by two burly guys. "Gideon is my husband. No badge required."

Of course the baby security officer was only doing his job. Someone he didn't recognize had stepped in front of the princess. How could Gideon fault him?

"I'm sorry, sir. Your Highness." Gideon saw the flash of the man's eyes from Alessandra to himself. He could practically feel the wheels in the guy's head turning. Wondering. How did someone like Gideon, in his jeans and cowboy boots, belong with her?

He'd always felt like an imposter, standing beside her at royal functions.

Alessandra was staring at him, and he worked to neutralize his expression. He didn't even know what mess of emotions might've been showing on his face.

"Are you blushing?"

"We need to get you in the car."

Their words tumbled over each other. Gideon didn't answer her question as he stepped into place beside her, forcing the security guy to fall in behind.

"Staff informed me there are a couple of photographers with long-range lenses near the fence." She murmured the words without really moving her lips, in full-on princess mode. Perfectly coifed and serene. They were only yards away from the SUV and Arnault.

Their last moments together and they couldn't even be private.

Emotion boiled up inside him. *Did you know he would be here?Are you happy to see him?*

He bit back the questions. He didn't even know if he had a right to ask them anymore.

What he wanted to do was take her hand. Right in front of Arnault and whoever had a camera out there. In front of the whole world. And whisk her away. Somewhere it'd be just the two of them. No royal duties. No ranch. Just Gideon and Allie.

Talk about pipe dreams.

"I wanted more time to talk," she murmured. They were within a few steps now.

Had she? He gave her the absolution he thought she wanted. "You've got a lot riding on this meeting. We both know how important it is."

It was true. For a lot of years, he'd been the sibling to be tasked with keeping his family's legacy alive. Alessandra's legacy was even bigger. She had a country depending on her.

He would never ask her to shirk her duty to the crown. It was a part of her. He'd known that before he'd gotten involved with her.

"I'll see you back at the palace," he said, though he didn't know whether or not that was true. Eloise and the palace staff held a lot of power of Alessandra's schedule. They might keep her so busy he couldn't get a minute in her presence.

She glanced from him to the first SUV. Or maybe Arnault. He saw her mouth move, but she was holding it in, whatever she wanted to say.

Fine.

"See ya, Allie." He didn't lean in and kiss her. Didn't take her hand, didn't make a single demand. He did his royal duty and got in the car.

And tried to shut off his imagination as to what kind of greeting she was getting from Arnault.

It was stupid to stay. He knew it.

But he couldn't get on a plane, not yet.

Giving up wasn't the Navy SEAL way.

Alessandra sat stiffly in the back of the SUV. There was one seat between her and Ronald, but it didn't feel like enough.

He'd started to greet her with a kiss on the cheek but Alessandra had stuck out her hand awkwardly between them, aware of Gideon. Was he watching them? Watching her?

Ronald had raised an expressive eyebrow, but she

found she didn't care. She wanted Gideon to know there was nothing more between them than simple friendship.

As the car rounded a bend, she couldn't help turning her head in an attempt to glimpse the SUV behind. It was silly. She couldn't see Gideon through the tinted windows anyway.

"Is everything all right?" Ronald asked.

She realized he held a computer tablet in the space between them, a passage from the proposal highlighted.

No. She closed her mouth over the initial response that wanted to escape.

She wasn't all right. Things were still uncertain between her and Gideon. They'd cleared the air of some of the hurts between them, but nothing had been resolved. Not really.

Now she smiled tightly. "I have some unfinished business with my husband."

Something shifted in Ronald's eyes. An expression there and gone so quickly... but one that made Alessandra wonder whether Gideon had been right. Surely Ronald didn't have romantic feelings for her. He'd never breathed a word.

There was something stiff about his smile. "You've been married a long time. He must understand what the crown demands of you."

He changed the subject, smoothly moving to show her the changes suggested after her administrative assistant had faxed over her penned-in edits from the plane.

But she couldn't focus on his words or the tablet. Instead, she found herself staring out the window.

He must understand.

Gideon had always understood the demands on her time. Wasn't he the one who had been playing on the floor with Maggie and Tirith when Alessandra had been late to celebrate his birthday? The girls had obviously had an elaborate celebration in mind, the room had been covered in streamers and balloons. The girls had screamed for her when she'd arrived. He'd glossed over the fact that she'd been in meetings all day across the border in their neighboring country.

She could still remember the tired lines around his eyes. Bea had been a toddler, demanding and needy. And yet Gideon had come to her and held her close, kissed her cheeks as the girls watched. He'd told her she was the only gift he ever wanted.

In those early years, they'd agreed that they didn't want nannies for their daughters, not if they could help it. Gideon had spent many exhausting days watching the girls, caring for them, while Alessandra did her duty for the crown. Often, he'd stood by her side at some gala or evening event. She was the only one who'd known how tired he was.

And then when Maggie had been so broken after the kidnapping, Gideon was the one who'd spent years of his life helping her heal. Alessandra was ashamed to admit now that she'd used her work for the crown to hide her own grief and fears and inadequacies.

She hadn't been strong enough to help Maggie. He had.

And he'd never asked for anything different. He'd never asked her to drop an event, even when the girls were sick with the flu and he hadn't slept in two days.

He understood the crown's demands. And he'd always put Alessandra and the girls first.

He was doing it again, even now.

He'd been shot. Given up a week of his time to protect her. She knew he would lay down his life for her.

And she'd gotten in the car with Ronald to work on this proposal. It was important work. It would impact her people and their lives.

But what about her life? What about Gideon's?

Hadn't he given up enough?

She felt an irrational fear that the second SUV would peel off and head back toward the airport. That

Gideon would be gone before she had a chance to speak to him again.

Ronald must've given up on having her attention, because he'd gone silent. Finally, they arrived at the castle. She was out of the car before her bodyguard could open the door.

Gideon exited his car and frowned at her for that. Didn't she know better?

But before she had a chance to go to him, to talk to him, an aide was at her side, pointing her toward the arched entrance. And Eloise, who was waiting just inside.

There was no refusing the Queen. The Queen rarely sought her out. They were both busy with their respective duties.

Alessandra barely had a chance to send an apologetic glance over her shoulder. Gideon's expression was shuttered, closed off. And then another aide stepped between them, and she lost sight of him.

Eloise jumped into an in-depth discussion of the proposal, one that Alessandra didn't dare drift away from. Her sister was demanding and impatient. And ultimately the ruler and protector of their kingdom.

Time passed as aides took rapid notes on their computers. Supper was brought in.

By the time Alessandra excused herself, it had grown late.

That didn't matter. She needed to see Gideon. But when she retired to her apartments within the castle, he was nowhere to be found.

Chapter Seven

Thirty-six hours after arriving in Glorvaird, Gideon was sequestered in a hotel room in a neighboring country.

The room was Alessandra's suite, and he passed through the living room into the bedroom. He pulled back the curtain just a bit. The window was ten stories high and had a view of the parking area, staffed by a valet, below.

It was a high-end hotel. The very hotel, in fact, where Alessandra and Ambassador Cain would meet to sign their finalized proposal in front of a bunch of television cameras.

Gideon didn't like the way this felt.

Maybe he should've gone home. Back to Texas.

"Dad? Did we get disconnected?"

Maggie's voice came from the cell phone he had pressed to his ear.

"I'm here, Mags. I heard you. Scarlette wants to sell off some of the cattle."

His niece—Carrie's daughter—and her husband co-ran the daily operations of the ranch now. They handled things when Maggie was called away to Glorvaird.

He let the curtain twitch back into place.

"Scarlette's got a good head on her shoulders."

Better than him. He felt foolish, being here.

He wasn't at this hotel in any official capacity. Not a part of the security team. And Alessandra sure as shootin' didn't know he was here.

He understood that Eloise had demanded her attention when they'd first arrived. But it'd been radio silence since.

No text, no phone call. She hadn't asked him to stay.

His wife couldn't have made it any clearer that she didn't want to see him.

So what was he doing here?

Nursing a broken heart, that's what.

"Dad? You okay?"

Had he made a noise? Maybe he'd sighed, like the sap he was. "I'm fine."

He strode back into the suite's sitting room. He'd

notified the security team about his presence, but Alessandra didn't know he planned to meet her here.

There was no window in this room and the lack of a visual to the outside bothered him. There was no balcony. No secondary escape route,. Which of the crown's security dunces had booked this room?

When he opened the door to the public hallway, he got the stink-eye from one of the two security guys outside. The hotel had claimed they'd blocked off access to this floor, but that was easy enough to overcome.

Gideon shut the door again, brain working.

"Why don't you just tell Mom you love her?"

Maggie's words through the phone line shocked him into stillness in the middle of a horrible hotel rug.

"What?"

Impatience blasted him through her sigh. "That's why you took off with her. Trying to protect her. Why you're in Glorvaird now."

He wasn't in Glorvaird, but he didn't say that. Maggie was too astute for her own good.

He stood frozen, emotion battering him. He'd kept busy since the interrupted ball so that he didn't have to face it. But Maggie wasn't letting him off the hook.

He closed his eyes and pressed a thumb and fore-finger into his eye sockets. It didn't help.

"I've always loved your mom." There was a relief in saying it. Admitting it to himself.

"When's the last time you said that to her?" Maggie asked.

He'd almost blurted it out in that little cabin, when she'd saved him from hypothermia. He was supposed to be the one rescuing her. She'd turned his life upside-down, from the very beginning. Made him realize what was truly important.

It had broken him, when they'd grown apart.

"Dad?"

He shook his head. His voice emerged rough. "I don't know, peanut."

"What do you really want?"

Her words galvanized him to go to the narrow desk on one wall and pull his laptop out of the leather carrying case. What he wanted right this second was for Alessandra to be safe. He'd managed to get it out of one of the old security guards he'd worked with before that she was due to arrive within the hour. He could spend that time memorizing an escape route. Just in case.

Because his gut was telling him something was wrong.

"If you want Mom back, you need to tell her how you really feel. Don't hold back."

He blinked away a hot layer of tears, quickly here

and gone. His daughter knew him. He didn't admit to his feelings easily. Never had. Had that stubbornness cost him years with Alessandra? Probably.

But Maggie might be onto something.

"It might not be that easy," he said as the schematics for the hotel popped up in his email inbox. "There are things that could keep us apart."

"So eliminate them." Maggie had always been the most practical of his daughters. And the most blood-thirsty. She loved a good revenge movie.

For a moment, he imagined getting Arnault out of his way in the most creative of ways. There was a visceral giddiness to the thought. But he blinked it away.

"One of those obstacles is your aunt," he said.

Maggie made a noise of understanding.

They both knew the strength of Alessandra's loyalty to the crown and the duties Eloise assigned her. He didn't think she'd ever walk away. It was part of who she was.

He personally thought Eloise took advantage of that. And Eloise knew that he thought it. It was part of why she didn't like him.

But it didn't mean the obstacle was insurmountable.

"The ranch can survive without you," Maggie said quietly. "You've put years of your life into it. If you want to stay in Glorvaird... I guess it comes down to the same question. What do you really want?"

His daughter might be a cowgirl, but she was also a royal, through and through. She could hold her own against any politician.

"When did you get to be the one dispensing advice?" he asked. If his voice was a little rough, he hoped she wouldn't notice through the cell phone connection.

She'd grown up when he wasn't watching. Fallen in love. He liked her husband well enough, even if he was a city slicker who barely knew how to ride. He treated Maggie right, and that was all that mattered.

"I just want you to be happy, Dad."

Now he had to blink a couple of times to get rid of that heat in his eyes. "Right back atcha, peanut."

She told him she loved him and rang off.

And he was left to stare at the hotel floor plans.

I just want you to be happy.

That's how he felt about Alessandra. If she was happy without him in her life, maybe the right thing was to walk away. Go back to the way things had been for the past fifteen years. Keep his broken heart to himself.

But he couldn't make the choice for her, could he? He was going to have to find some iota of courage and tell her how he felt. Find out whether she was really done with him.

Over the past week they'd spent together, he'd thought he felt their relationship opening back up again.

But once she'd stepped foot in Glorvaird, she'd gone silent.

Maybe that was his answer.

But he was a stubborn cowboy. Had been his whole life. He was going to make her say it to his face.

But first, he had to make sure she survived the night.

"You look different," Bea said.

The video connection on Alessandra's phone flickered momentarily and then stabilized. She was riding in the back of a black Town Car, this one reinforced so it was as secure as possible. She was alone in the backseat —the first time she'd been alone since she'd awakened this morning. One bodyguard drove, while another sat beside him in the passenger seat.

"My stylist hasn't changed," she told her daughter.

She looked past the image on the phone to the proposal still in her lap. The final version. She was meant to meet with the ambassador in an hour. They were only minutes from the hotel.

"That's not what I meant. Mother—do you need to go?"

She felt a faint flush rise under her skin as Bea called her on her distraction. She locked her eyes on the screen.

"I can talk for a few more minutes. What did you mean?"

"There are fewer lines around your mouth," her daughter said with a smirk. "Have you been smiling more?"

Alessandra felt her cheeks pull into a too-false smile even as she answered her daughter. "I smile."

Bea lifted an eyebrow.

"I smile." This time her voice held a note of petulance.

In the front seat, one of the guards shifted and Alessandra straightened in her seat automatically, self-conscious.

"I was afraid you and Dad would argue the entire time."

"We did."

But the memory that popped into Alessandra's head wasn't from those tense first few hours. It was Gideon watching her as she'd knelt over a basket of puppies and giggled like a young schoolgirl.

"You're smiling now," Bea pointed out helpfully.

Alessandra strove to control her expression. She didn't know what was wrong. She'd struggled to contain her emotions all day. She'd nearly snapped at a poor staffer who'd done nothing but moved a bit too slowly when Alessandra had hoped to have a few minutes to locate her husband.

"Are you seeing Dad tonight?"

Alessandra's gaze flicked to the front of the car and back to the phone. "I don't know. I'll be at this trade meeting for hours. I haven't been able to get in touch with him."

She'd called once. He hadn't answered, and she hadn't left a voicemail. It had seemed too impersonal after everything they'd weathered the past week.

He might even be at the airport right now.

The thought of Gideon leaving, walking away again, brought tears pricking her eyes. She gave her daughter her profile as she tried to collect herself.

"I've been busy since we touched down yesterday." It was a flimsy excuse, and they both knew it.

"You're a princess of Glorvaird," Bea said quietly. "You're in control of your own diary."

It was true. And it was courageous of her daughter to call her out on it. There was an element of bowing to Eloise's wishes. And a whisper of her Father's voice echoing in her memory, demanding she put aside all else for the crown.

But that wasn't all of it.

"I'm frightened," she admitted in a whisper, "that we've hurt each other one too many times."

Gideon hadn't shown his face after Ronald had been waiting at the airport. Last night after Eloise had finally been finished with her, Alessandra had pored over paparazzi photos for hours.

Gideon was right. Ronald often put her in a more compromising position than was true. Leaning in closer than a friend. Watching her with a certain look on his face. Had he done it on purpose? She wanted to give him the benefit of the doubt. Perhaps some of the photos looked how they did because of a camera angle.

But perhaps there was a portion of blame to be borne by herself, too. She'd chosen to go to lunch or out for coffee after their official meetings were over. A part of her had craved the attention. Her own husband didn't want her, but Ronald always listened. Was there to share a meal.

She'd done Gideon wrong. And she hadn't apologized, not really. She'd told him the truth, that there was only friendship between them, that she'd never betrayed Gideon's trust. But she'd also made excuses instead of addressing the hurt her husband had admitted to.

"Did you ever think maybe Dad's scared, too?"

A tiny laugh hiccuped out of her. "Your father? He's never scared."

Even as she said the words, she remembered a long-ago time, waking up from a hazy, poison-induced coma. Gideon had been at her side, and he had been deathly frightened. Of losing her.

Had he just become better at hiding his fears over the years?

They'd both learned to hide from each other.

And they'd suffered for it.

Even now, the urge to put things off rose inside her. It would be easy to simply fall back into old routines. Go back to the way things were.

"I don't want to be estranged any longer." The words were out before she'd fully thought them through. But once she'd spoken, she felt the rightness of them.

She wanted Gideon back in her life. She wanted the closeness they'd once had.

She knew it would be a fight, but it would be worth it.

"I'll call you soon," she promised her daughter before they rang off. Then she realized they'd been idling at the curb for long minutes.

"Just waiting for the interior security team to give us the all clear," one of the guards responded when she asked what was going on.

It gave her time to dial Gideon's number. She would ask him not to leave. To give her a chance to see him.

She would beg, if that's what it took.

But his phone went to voicemail.

She stared at the shadowy building that stretched up to the sky. It was beautiful and gothic and historical. Gideon would say there weren't enough lights. Too many shadows, too many places to hide.

It sent a shiver of unease through her.

She had her security team, but the reminder wasn't as comforting as it would've been with her husband by her side.

Even through the assassination attempt at Maggie's ball, she hadn't been afraid. Not really. She'd known Gideon wouldn't let any harm come to her.

He'd always put her first.

She had to do her duty. Sign this proposal in front of a bunch of cameras. But that was it. After that, she would find Gideon. Hire a private detective if he didn't go back to the ranch.

She needed him.

Chapter Eight

Something was wrong.

It was there in the tense silence of the three bodyguards escorting her to the hotel room to wait. They would convene in the conference room within the hour.

Alessandra jumped when someone slammed a door nearby.

The bodyguard on her right reached beneath his suit jacket for his weapon.

That wasn't good.

There was the room. Weren't there supposed to be two guards outside?

Prickles ran up the back of her neck. What would Gideon advise her to do?

"Call for backup," she ordered the man on her right.

There'd been several new hires in the past months, and she didn't know his name.

Her heart raced. Her palms dampened.

And then the door to her suite opened.

She gasped as a tall form filled the doorway.

"Gideon." She breathed his name.

Gideon was here. He would—

He took in the three guards with one of his thunder-cloud frowns.

"Do you trust me?" he murmured.

There was no question. "Of course."

He didn't pull her into the room, but stepped into the hall, taking her arm and pulling her away from the suite, in the same direction they'd been walking.

"Hale!" One of the security guards wasn't happy about it.

"She'll be a sitting duck in that room. There's no other exit." He let his words encompass the entire team, who had no choice but to stay at her side when she kept walking.

They approached a corner where the hallway split into a T. Gideon held back as one of the guards moved forward to check both directions.

At the momentary pause, Alessandra reached down to remove one of her three-inch heels. She swayed as Gideon's hand came underneath her arm to steady her. She switched feet and took off the other shoe.

"Where are the guards from the hallway?" she shot the commanding question at the bodyguard to her left, François, who was the lead today, and Gideon shot her an appreciative look.

The man shook his head as she clutched her shoes in one hand, leaving the other free.

The bodyguard in front of them motioned them forward.

Alessandra's stomach twisted. Something still felt wrong—

Gideon ushered her forward. Just as they cleared the corner and turned right, a door thunked closed somewhere down the hallway they'd just come from.

The guard behind her peeled away at a look from François. Gideon pushed her into a run.

"This floor is supposed to be completely empty," he whispered fiercely.

"Where's the backup?" she demanded of François.

Another appreciative glance from Gideon. She didn't have time to soak in his praise that she'd asked for reinforcements.

They reached the end of the hallway as sounds of a scuffle then a pop like a muffled gunshot sounded.

Terror smothered her in an instant. Her brain

wanted to spiral back to the moments at the gala, or further, to thirty years ago when an assassin had nearly killed her.

Gideon seemed to know it, and his arm came around her waist. He steadied her and put himself between her and whatever was happening behind them at the same time. There was only one doorway at this end of the building. A stairwell.

The bodyguard ahead yanked it open and went inside with gun drawn.

"It's clear—"

He didn't even get the word out before Gideon pushed her inside.

The stairwell was well-lit, white fluorescent lights buzzing overhead. Was that good or bad?

"Down," Gideon said decisively.

One of the guards stayed behind at the door, which meant that only one remained with Gideon and Alessandra.

She started down the stairs between the two men. She had a stitch in her side from the short run and now the stairs. Her husband wasn't even breathing hard. But she hadn't forgotten he was injured.

"Your side," she panted.

"Ssh."

She sent him a scathing look. He grinned at her, though she saw the worry behind his easy expression.

He was trying to keep her from spiraling into that place of fear and frozenness.

"I'm fine," he mouthed when they reached the next landing.

She didn't know whether to believe him, didn't have a choice as he motioned the guard to keep going.

They'd started on the tenth floor. Surely this stairwell wasn't the best place to be—

A shot rang out from above them.

She flinched even as Gideon pushed her into a ducking position near the wall and covered her body with his own.

She half-stumbled, half-ran down the next flight of stairs.

Another shot rang out. Gideon dove for the exit that would lead them out onto the fifth floor.

She scurried through, trying not to make any noise. She hadn't dared look. Had the gunman been on the tenth floor? Had he somehow seen them exit?

The hallway was empty except for a young mother and her toddler at the far end, who looked startled to see them.

"Police are at the lobby level," François said. "They're locking down the hotel."

But the gunman was still behind them.

Gideon looked into her eyes. "Can you run some more?"

"Of course." She might wish she'd hired a better personal trainer, but she would.

He flew down the hallway, propelling her with him. François was at their heels.

He stopped at the elevator, mashed the button.

Gideon never chose an elevator. He'd once claimed you could never know who was waiting when the door opened.

Were things this desperate?

The doors opened, the car was miraculously empty.

Gideon pointed to some kind of card reader on the panel as they stepped inside. "Scan your pass." He aimed his words at François.

The guard took a key card from an inner pocket. Her security team had been granted access to every space in the hotel. The guard stepped off the elevator as Gideon pushed the button for a basement floor. Why there?

The doors closed, and they were alone.

"What are you even doing here?" she asked, still breathing hard, clutching the elevator railing with one hand.

Her husband had the grace to look slightly sheepish. Was he blushing beneath his tan?

"Please don't tell me you only came to protect me."

Not that she was ungrateful for his protection right now. If he hadn't followed his instinct and gotten her away from that hotel room, she would've been stuck inside—possibly facing—the barrel of a gun.

And then his expression changed to determined. "We've got some unfinished business between us, don't we?"

Her heart leaped. "There are a lot of things I need to tell you."

The elevator's motion started to slow. Gideon glanced at the numbers flashing on the wall display. "Tell me when we're safe."

"No."

She surprised him. Surprised herself.

"I'm not waiting to tell you I still love you."

He only had a beat to stare at her in surprise before the doors opened on a long utilitarian hallway. Not a space open to the public.

Gideon went right back into soldier mode. He escorted her off the elevator then nodded to the first set of doors, a swinging double door.

She followed him inside to a busy kitchen.

And a whole heap of security guards filing in from the opposite side.

Pure relief that made her burst into tears.

* * *

Gideon watched as Alessandra lost control of her emotions in a spectacular way. His wife usually had iron control over herself. The fact that they were in public made it even more surprising.

He was aware that the attacker could still be out there, but when she turned into his arms, he scooped her in close. He turned his shoulder to shield her from anyone who might use their phone as a camera. She took a hitching breath and shuddered.

I love you.

His heart was pounding, but not from the danger. Not when Alessandra had just told him the words he longed to hear.

He and his wife were surrounded by royal guards almost instantly. He recognized Roberto, a man only a few years younger than himself, with whom he'd worked closely years ago. The man tapped his cheek, drawing Gideon's attention to the earpiece.

"They've apprehended him. He claims he was

working alone, but we'll sweep the hotel. Local police are en route."

A lone gunman. Gideon felt some of his tension drain away.

Alessandra was still trembling in his arms, though she'd composed herself and now swept one hand across her cheeks.

"I imagine you still want to meet with the ambassador," he said quietly.

She glanced up, the tip of her nose still red. She was so close. All he had to do was lean forward, close those few inches...

But he didn't. This was real life. Alessandra was still a member of the royal family, and now a TV camera had entered the room. Some reporter must've gotten wind of the guards' movements and followed them.

Two guards were already ushering the cameraman and reporter out, but Gideon knew better than to make a spectacle. Even though he dearly wanted to.

Alessandra took a half-step back, and he let his hands fall away.

"Is it safe?" she asked, her words encompassing both him and the guard.

"We're sweeping the conference room floor first. The ambassador is already here, and his security team is frantic to ensure his safety."

"I'd like to sign today," Alessandra said. "This is too important to delay."

He'd known she would say that.

As the guard faded back, she glanced up at Gideon almost shyly. "I worried you'd gone to the airport."

His heart leaped. Worried was good. "No airport."

"No. Because...?"

"Because there are things I need to say."

She was looking at him with such a hopeful, warm look that he wanted to sweep her in his arms and kiss her.

And of course, an aide chose that moment to interrupt. "Your Highness, they're ready for you."

Duty called.

It was only a matter of minutes before Alessandra was ushered into a large conference room. He remained at her side, mostly because of how tightly she was gripping his hand. Inside the room, a dais showed where she would stand, along with the ambassador. There were fewer photographers and reporters than he'd expected. And a larger security force, the men in dark suits outnumbering the press.

He attempted to let go of Alessandra's hand as she neared the stage, to fade back and stand against the wall, out of the limelight.

She turned to him. And didn't let go.

"Come up there with me."

He shook his head. "My place—"

"Is right next to me."

Maybe she was still frightened.

"Not because of any threats." Or maybe she'd read his mind. "Because I need you beside me."

His heart thumped hard. "What about—" He cut himself off as he glanced to the stage. There wasn't room on that little platform for both him and Arnault.

Except Arnault was nowhere in sight.

"There's a lot I need to talk to you about," she murmured. "He isn't here. And he won't be. I want it to be you, standing beside me."

Eloise wouldn't be happy. But Gideon was done arguing. If Alessandra was going to fight for them, he was too.

He wasn't dressed for the event. Alessandra and the ambassador wore tailored pantsuits, and he was dressed in jeans and a T-shirt. Ruining the photo opp. But Alessandra didn't seem to care.

She introduced him to the ambassador, who shook his hand and took his measure with a gaze. Cameras flashed.

Gideon stood back a bit as they signed the document. He was proud of his wife and the work she did. He could feel it oozing from his pores.

In his pocket, his phone buzzed. He resisted the urge to check it. This spectacle wouldn't last much longer. The guards for both the ambassador and Alessandra were antsy. They wanted both high-profile marks out of the public eye after the thwarted attack.

It was only a matter of minutes before he and Alessandra were ushered out through an underground parking garage and into the back of a limo with darkly tinted windows.

To his surprise, she asked for privacy. Slid the divider up that would separate them from the driver.

But she was dialing her phone.

He used the moment to dig his own phone out of his pocket. Tirith had texted him.

You're standing up with Mother!

While he was holding the phone, it buzzed with another text. Bea. *I expect to hear details.*

He loved his daughters.

Alessandra had the phone pressed to her ear. "I need to speak to her."

She glanced at him with a trembling smile.

His curiosity was piqued.

"Eloise, I'm pulling back on my duties."

His heart went into his throat as he registered her words.

"Valentin can take some of the committee work. My

marriage deserves more of me than I've been able to give. I'll have Clara clear some time for us to sit down and talk through what that will look like."

He was shaking his head as she rang off, disbelief rampant.

"You didn't have to do that," he said.

She tossed the phone on the cushion beside her. "Yes, I did." She motioned to his phone with a curious look on her face. He tilted the phone so she could see Bea's text.

"Tirith texted too. Sounds like the girls are hoping for reconciliation."

"That's what I'm hoping for as well."

The vulnerable words cost her. He saw it in the downward tilt of her chin, the clench of her hand in her lap.

It was his turn to be vulnerable. "I should've run after you a long time ago. Left the ranch behind and moved here permanently. But if I'm not too late, that's what I plan to do now."

Beautiful hope was shining from her tear-filled eyes.

He did what felt natural and slid his arm around her shoulders. With his other hand, he brushed some hair out of her eyes. Swallowed hard. "I've been so stupid. I should've told you every day how much I love you. I never stopped, even though I lost the words. You'll never know how sorry I am for that."

One tear slipped free and rolled down her cheek. He brushed it away.

"I'm sorry too," she whispered. "I love you. I never stopped either."

Joy and warmth flowed up inside him, filling every crack.

He leaned in and kissed her, and it was just the same as always—like coming home. Like everything he'd always wanted.

Chapter Nine

Alessandra zipped the simple white sheath dress before taking a settling breath and looking in the full-length mirror.

Her hair had been pulled back in a French twist. Her makeup was natural, the way Gideon preferred. The tiniest nerves buzzing along beneath her skin didn't show.

"Mother?" A knock at the door. Tirith.

"Come in, dear." Oof. Her voice was shaking, just the slightest bit. She took another settling breath.

Tirith slipped inside the room. The secluded cottage was sequestered in the Glorvaird foothills, private, and as beautiful as a wild rose garden. Alessandra and Gideon had rented the entire space, creating a haven for their family for this momentous weekend.

"Are you nervous?" Tirith wore a teal calf-length dress that accentuated her figure.

"No." Alessandra ignored the butterflies tickling her stomach at the denial. "Why should I be?"

She and Gideon had been together nearly every moment of every day since that terrifying week almost a year ago.

Gideon had stayed with her in Glorvaird, turning over the ranch operations to Maggie and Scarlette. Alessandra had taken a step back in the number of commitments she accepted at Eloise's behest.

They shared meals together. Slept in the same room. Traveled together.

She'd only been this incandescently happy in the early days of their marriage.

"Why should I be?" she muttered to the mirror, lest Tirith see that she actually was.

"You shouldn't." Tirith came to stand close behind her, offering a quick hug and then stepping back slightly, still visible in the mirror's reflection. "You love Dad. And he loves you."

He told her so every day. When she woke up to find him watching her from his pillow, sleepy and content. When they slow danced together without music on the balcony outside her rooms in the castle. In little notes left in her briefcase, and through his touch when he kissed her.

"And today was your idea." Tirith offered the reminder with a faint smirk that quickly turned into her lips pressing into a white line. She inhaled through her nose as Alessandra whirled in concern. Her daughter had gone a familiar faint shade of green.

"I wondered why there were saltine crackers and ginger candies left in such a sweet display on my dresser when we checked in." She pointed Tirith to the long, low dresser along one wall. Her daughter hurried over and wasted no time in unwrapping one of the candies and popping it into her mouth.

A few moments and a few deep breaths later, Tirith had regained a bit of color.

Alessandra raised her brows. "Something you want to tell me?"

Tirith shook her head slightly. "No. Edward and I agreed that we weren't going to tell anyone this weekend. We want this time to be about you and Dad."

What a sweet sentiment.

She crossed the room to hug her daughter gently. "Congratulations. What does Edward think?"

"He's over the moon," Tirith admitted, the words slightly muffled in her mother's shoulder. "I can't believe the staff delivered my things to your room."

Alessandra felt the prick of tears as she stepped back, though she still held on to Tirith's shoulders. "I'm so very proud of you."

Of course, that was the moment that Gideon chose to knock on the door and then step inside. "You about ready?"

He took in her closeness with Tirith in a glance and a smile kicked up one corner of his mouth.

"I just need my earrings." Alessandra let go of Tirith, who discreetly moved to the dresser and slipped several candies into an invisible pocket in her dress.

From the nightstand, Alessandra saw their daughter kiss Gideon's cheek on her way out the door.

Alessandra slipped one earring in, then the other, feeling Gideon's gaze on her the entire time.

"I should've sent Maggie after you."

She cocked one eyebrow. "If you compare me to cattle to be rounded up..."

She left the threat hanging, a smile slipping free.

His eyes were warm as she approached. "Nah. Maybe a docile little sheep."

She laughed in surprise. He caught her waist in his hands. "Careful. You look so delicious that if you come any closer, I won't want to let you go."

She blushed. It shouldn't have been possible, not at her age. "Gideon."

His eyes sparked. "It's true. And you've got a room full of people waiting for you."

That was a slight exaggeration. She'd asked for their girls to be here, along with their husbands. Bea was seeing someone, and it was serious. The young man had asked for an audience with Alessandra and Gideon only a week ago to seek their blessing to propose to Bea. He'd been invited too.

An intimate ceremony. A renewing of their vows with the people they loved best.

"You ready?" Gideon asked.

They'd been through the fire, and she'd almost lost him, this dear man she loved. The ceremony today was an affirmation of every promise she'd made in their wedding ceremony years ago.

She still chose him.

And she was ready for what life would bring, with him at her side.

"Let's go."

Thank you for reading HIS FOREVER PRINCESS. I hope you loved Gideon and Alessandra's reunion romance. If you want to read about another heroine on the run and the man who protects her, try HIS SMALL

TOWN GIRL:

She's sweet and wholesome. And hiding something.

He's back home, resurrecting old ghosts.

One of them is going to get hurt.

Molly arrives in Sutter's Hollow out of gas and out of options. The rundown ranch seems like a perfect place to hide. Except the man who owns it seems just as dangerous as what's chasing her.

Cord's mantra growing up? *Get out of Sutter's Hollow.* Now he's back in town, but only long enough to get rid of his grandma's ball and chain—the ranch. He doesn't need a complication like Molly, who reminds him of an injured baby bird. He's no protector. So why can't he tell her to get lost?

Also by Lacy Williams

Wagon Train Matches series (historical romance)

A Trail So Lonesome

Trail of Secrets

A Trail Untamed

Wind River Hearts series (historical romance)

Marrying Miss Marshal

Counterfeit Cowboy

Cowboy Pride

The Homesteader's Sweetheart

Courted by a Cowboy

Roping the Wrangler

Return of the Cowboy Doctor

The Wrangler's Inconvenient Wife

A Cowboy for Christmas

Her Convenient Cowboy

Her Cowboy Deputy

Catching the Cowgirl

The Cowboy's Honor

Winning the Schoolmarm

The Wrangler's Ready-Made Family

Christmas Homecoming

Heart of Gold

Sutter's Hollow series (contemporary romance)

His Small-Town Girl

Secondhand Cowboy

The Cowgirl Next Door

Cowboy Fairytales series (contemporary fairytale romance)

Once Upon a Cowboy

Cowboy Charming

The Toad Prince

The Beastly Princess

The Lost Princess

Kissing Kelsey

Courting Carrie

Stealing Sarah

Keeping Kayla

Melting Megan

The Other Princess

The Prince's Matchmaker

The True Princess

His Forever Princess

Hometown Sweethearts series (contemporary romance)

Kissed by a Cowboy

Love Letters from Cowboy

Mistletoe Cowboy

The Bull Rider

The Brother

The Prodigal

Cowgirl for Keeps

Jingle Bell Cowgirl

Heart of a Cowgirl

3 Days with a Cowboy

Prodigal Cowgirl

Soldier Under the Mistletoe

The Nanny's Christmas Wish

The Rancher's Unexpected Gift

Someone Old

Someone New

Someone Borrowed

Someone Blue (newsletter subscribers only)

Ten Dates

Next Door Santa

Always a Bridesmaid

Love Lessons

Not in a Series

Wagon Train Sweetheart (historical romance)